for my mother, of course

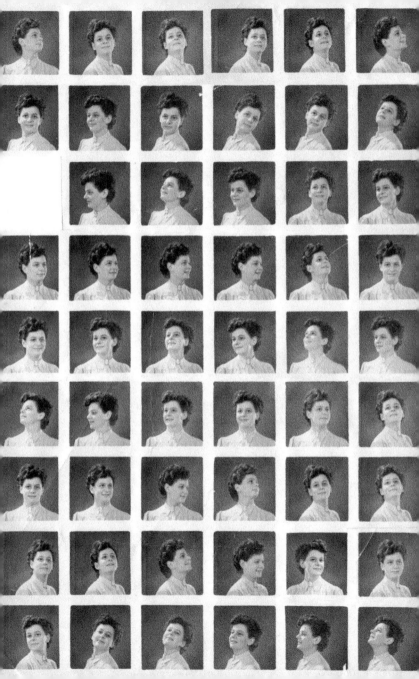

By the same author:

Too Raucous For A Chorus
By Bus
Living Locally
Em & Me
The Book Remembers Everything

ERICA VAN HORN is an American artist (and writer, editor, printer, bookmaker, and publisher) long transplanted to Ireland where she runs Coracle Press with her husband Simon Cutts. Her outsider's acumen is trained on the minutiae of daily life, collecting visual and textual details of what is often overlooked or seemingly insignificant.

I Have Been Making Books Since the Day President Kennedy was Shot, an exhibition at Franklin Furnace, NYC in 1986, highlighted books she had produced up until that date. *We Still Have the Telephone* is her most recent title.

WE STILL HAVE
THE TELEPHONE

Erica Van Horn

the quick brown fox

LesFugitives

We Still Have the Telephone

My mother and I have been writing her obituary. We have been working on it for several years now. Before we started, she had already begun the project with my older sister. She wants to get it right. After my sister died, the job of rewriting and tweaking and editing fell to me. If something happens to me, my younger sister will have to take on the task. The newspaper charges fifty cents a word for obituaries. My mother is not bothered by how much it costs because she will not be having a casket nor a funeral. She will not even have a quiet cremation. She has donated her body to science and after they are done with her she is not worried about what happens to any bits that remain. Her current concern is that her body might already be too old to be of interest to the research department. There is a second worry that because she lives alone, she might die and no one will notice her absence right away. The medical school only want bodies if they can get them within a certain number of hours after death. My mother hates waste. She does not want her body to go to waste. She wants it to be useful to science. At last count, her obituary was six hundred and nineteen words but I know that we have not yet arrived at our final draft.

Each time I visit, my mother insists that we set aside a morning to work on the obituary. Which we do. We then go out to lunch and discuss all that we have been doing, but over lunch we discuss it without pens and paper. It is a different conversation over lunch. In the final days before I leave to fly home, I type up our most recent draft and I print it out for her to peruse. She sits down at the table and immediately begins to tweak it. By the time I am actually departing, she has already made a lot of changes. When I get home, I re-type it and I print it out again and I send the newest version to her in the post. This is the version she will work on with a pencil and small careful changes until my next visit.

I wonder if I will ever see my mother again.

Over the last year, a friend and I have discussed the possibility that we might never see our mothers again. My friend's mother died yesterday. She was one hundred and three years old and she died in her own bed in her own home with her son nearby. She woke up in the night and she told him that she wanted to go back to sleep, so he gave her a little hug and she went back to sleep and then she did not wake up. My friend had not seen her mother since February. I have not seen my mother since last October. My mother is only ninety-four which is young compared to one hundred and three. It did not make any difference at all that my friend was living in Scotland and that her mother was in England. She was a mere train journey away. My mother is on the other side of the Atlantic Ocean. With the current pandemic, all distances have become equal. All distances are impossible. We cannot go anywhere. We cannot go to anyone.

The latest version of the obituary opens with the fact that as a child in London during the Second World War, my mother was required to carry a gas mask. If she, or any other child, arrived at school without their gas mask they were sent home to collect it. She likes beginning her obituary with this information as she feels it makes her life stand out a little from any of the others described in the New Hampshire newspaper. This kind of detail makes my mother's obituary a bit foreign. She feels that by being different, it is special. She was not born in Winnisquam or Sunapee or Penacook. She was not born in New Hampshire. My mother wants her life to be reported in her own words and with her own emphasis on those facts that she wants remembered.

I have been trying to remember things about my mother now, while she is still alive. I fear that once she is dead, my memories will take on a different patina. She wants to tell her life in her own way. I need to remember it my way. I need to hold on to the parts of her that I find endearing and I need to remind myself of those things that I find annoying. My mother is interested in her version of facts. I am interested in details. I am collecting the things that I might forget.

My mother never makes a hard-boiled egg without writing on the shell as soon as the egg has cooled. Eggs are always written upon with a pencil, never with a pen. If there are three eggs they might be labelled Wynken, Blynken and Nod. Two eggs might be Abbott and Costello. Or Tom and Jerry. Or Victoria and Albert. The number of eggs will be labelled with names that come in twos or threes or whatever quantity of eggs that she has hard-boiled. She labels the eggs even if she is alone at home and she is planning to eat them herself immediately. She labels the eggs once they are cooked and cooling on the counter so that no-one can possibly mistake a hard-boiled egg for a fresh egg. She labels the eggs by writing names on their shells with a pencil because that is what she has always done.

Until recently my mother felt it wasteful to hard-boil a single egg even if she only wanted to eat one egg herself. The smallest number of eggs she would allow herself to hard-boil was two. It was okay to boil one egg if it was for eating immediately as a soft-boiled egg, but a hard-boiled egg had to be cooked together with a second egg. The second one could be put into the refrigerator and eaten tomorrow, but it was a waste of water, heat and time to hard-boil a single egg.

Now, suddenly, at the age of ninety-four, for some reason I do not know, my mother tells me that she has decided that it is permissible for her to hard-boil one egg. It is no longer necessary to boil two. However there is a condition on this boiling of a single egg and that is that the solitary egg must be labelled, with pencil, as the eggs have always been labelled with pencil, but her new rule is that the single egg must be labelled with a name that starts with the letters H and B. Hard Boiled. Hillaire Belloc. Halle Berry. Heinrich Böll. Harry Belafonte. Even if the egg is to be consumed immediately it must be named and labelled before it is cracked and peeled and eaten.

I cannot remember how old she was when my mother confided to me that she hates buttons. I assumed that her dislike of buttons was a result of age. I thought possibly she had arthritis or some other stiffness in her fingers. I thought that her extreme hatred of buttons might come from an inability to button and to unbutton. I asked her as diplomatically as I could if perhaps this was the reason for her strong dislike of buttons. She assured me that neither age nor pain had anything to do with it. She said that as a child she had no opinion one way or the other, but as an adult she has always hated buttons. She told me that she has hated buttons for as long as she can remember.

My mother is outraged. We spoke on the telephone today. She could barely contain her anger. The reason for her outrage is because the world is ganging up against the use of plastic and specifically against plastic straws. There is a real uproar and she is taking it all personally. As usual. She uses plastic straws to drink as it helps her to control the excessive choking and the reflux in her oesophagus and throat. She has a large supply of plastic straws. They are all brought home from restaurants. She washes them and she re-uses them. She cuts some in half and some of them she leaves long. She could easily buy a packet of drinking straws but she likes to recycle and she especially likes to use things that are free. She has an enormous supply of straws. She has enough straws to last her for the next thirty years, but my mother now feels terrified that plastic straws will be banned and even though she washes her straws and uses each one multiple times she fears that she might run out of them before she dies.

On Sunday mornings my mother percolates freshly ground decaffeinated coffee and she drinks it from a fine white porcelain cup and saucer. The rest of the week she uses mugs, but she feels that Sunday morning calls for a little ritual. Her Sunday is not about religion. Sunday is about getting the New York Times. Receiving the Sunday edition of the New York Times is not always possible so far north. There is not much demand for it in rural New Hampshire. Sometimes it is not delivered until Tuesday, but she anticipates and hopes for its arrival every Sunday.

We were not allowed to chew gum when we were children. My mother had no time for people who chewed gum. By the time I was old enough to choose for myself whether or not I wanted to chew gum, I did not even consider it because I had completely accepted the belief that chewing gum was a vile American habit. I knew that walking down the street with a wad of gum being endlessly mashed between my teeth would make me look like a cow. I knew that chewing gum with an open mouth was the ugliest thing on earth. At the age of ninety, my mother was instructed by her doctor to chew gum for her throat and her oesophagus and her choking problems. The mechanism of the chewing helps to keep her saliva moving and that is somehow a useful and necessary thing. She chews her sugarless gum like a little mouse, carefully and with small quick little nibbles up and down and up and down always with her lips tightly closed. No one can watch my mother and believe that she chews gum for pleasure.

Some mothers are full of helpful household hints. They have books with titles like TIPS & WRINKLES so that they know how to remove any stain or scratch or how to sort out any kitchen disaster. My mother did not have many hints to pass on to us. Her recent advice to me regarding a moth infestation among my sweaters was that I should wear a shirt of the same colour underneath my sweater. She explained that if a sweater is black I should wear a black shirt underneath it. That is the trick. She swears that no one will ever notice the holes. Other people recommend lavender and placing sweaters in the freezer to eliminate moth eggs. My mother's solution is not a solution. It is a trick to pretend that the moths never happened. I think it is because her own mother was not the kind of mother who had special answers and solutions. My mother did not learn her mother's tricks along the way so she did not have any tricks to pass along to my sisters and I. She did not learn things like that along the way, so we did not learn things like that along the way.

The dining room has always been the centre of activity in the house. It is never a simple thing to sit down in the dining room. There are eight or nine or maybe ten chairs in the room, and each chair has a specific function. My mother sits in one chair for breakfast. At lunch and dinner she sits in the chair on the opposite side of the table from her breakfast chair. There are cushions on each of these chairs. Everywhere else there are a lot of different kinds of piles of things. There are piles of newspapers on three of the chairs. One holds sections of the Sunday edition of the New York Times which have not yet been read, or sections which may need to be returned to for further perusal. Another chair holds copies of the local and state newspapers such as the Concord Monitor and the Suncook Valley Sun. These have probably already been read but they cannot be released yet because there might be an article to return to or a piece that needs to be cut out. The third chair holds those papers and magazines that are on their way out to the recycling pile in the kitchen. Those papers on the third chair, which is a narrow chair in front of the window looking out onto the porch, have been thoroughly read or they were not read and they were just discarded immediately because they are things that are never read, like the sports pages.

The newspapers are everywhere on every chair but they are tidy.

SHE LOVED PENNIES. My mother often announces that she would love to have this as the epitaph carved on her gravestone, if only she were the kind of person to have a gravestone. But with no grave and no stone, she does not know where she might use this declarative sentence. So far she has not found the appropriate way to fit it into the obituary, but we are not done with the obituary yet. It may well appear there before we are finished.

Every Christmas my sister makes my mother something out of pennies. One year it was a sign with the numbers 12-25-17 written out with shiny pennies glued onto a bright red board. My mother loved it. She loved it but she could barely look at it. She was thrilled with all of the coins but she could not wait to pick it all apart and to rub the rubber cement off the back of each penny. Her immediate response was to turn the pennies back from decoration into money. Then she could deposit them in the bank.

She is always saving. It used to be pennies but now it has moved up the coin ladder. If we are eating lunch in a diner, and I put down a pile of change to tip the waitress, my mother snatches up the change and replaces it with dollar bills. She has the dollar bills ready. She is quivering with anticipation about the coins she can gather. It is no longer about an exchange. It used to be that she would hand over a one-dollar bill for my one dollar in coins. That does not happen anymore. She just grabs the coins. She started out by offering to take pennies off anyone who had some going spare. Then she moved to nickels and dimes. She now includes quarters in her compulsive collecting. She gathers up the change and she waits until someone drives her to the bank and then she deposits her little bags of coins into her bank account. Ever since she learned that the bank has a machine to automatically count coins, she no longer waits until her collections add up to an even amount. She is always trying to make a little more money.

The key for the back door is labelled B.D.

My mother takes a particular interest and delight in numbers and dates that look good or that add up in a tidy fashion. On the tenth of October she sent me a message:

> I meant to get this to you earlier.
> 10-10-20
> Not many dates are this memorable or delightful!

It would have made no difference if I had been alerted to this date sooner. There was nothing at all to be done with the information. It was something for her to anticipate with pleasure and to enjoy on the day.

Envelopes demand a special ritual. When an envelope has been filled with a letter or a card or a bill to be paid, it is addressed and the return address is neatly rubber-stamped in the upper left-hand corner. A postage stamp is placed on the upper right-hand corner and the envelope is left on the marble-topped chest to be taken to the post office or to the nearest mailbox. The one thing that is not done is that the flap of the envelope is not glued down. At some point in their old age, it became an agreement between my parents that my mother piled up any envelopes filled and ready to go and my father came along later and licked all of the flaps to seal them. My mother does all of the bill paying. She has always been in charge of the finances and the paying out. I think this envelope licking was a way for her to include my father in the process of taking care of things, especially as he got older and was increasingly oblivious to what was happening around him. My father has been dead for nine years now. Mail is still placed on the corner of the marble-topped chest for the final sealing. As a result of my father's death, there is a tendency for letters to be posted without them ever being properly closed. My mother fails to lick the flaps and my father is not there to do it. The people at the post office in the village now take a quick look at my mother's envelopes to ensure that all of her flaps are stuck down.

I was nine years old and I had a terrible cold. My mother kept me home from school for the day. In the late morning, she made tea and we sat together in the living room. I was bundled up under a blanket. The room was flooded with sunlight. The day felt bright and warm even though it was winter and it was bitterly cold and snowy outside. The telephone rang. My mother received a long-distance telephone call from London. It was her youngest brother ringing to inform her that their father had died. She cried. She sat in the chair opposite me and she wept. It was not the first time I had seen my mother weeping. She frequently cried in films when there was a sad moment. She was moved to tears when horrible events were reported on the news. She wept for injustices and tragedies in parts of the world where suffering was rife. This was a different kind of crying. I was unable to say a word as I watched her. She was not exactly sobbing but her entire body was involved in the crying. I was sitting close by, but she was all alone. I was exactly where I had been before the telephone call, but I was miles away. I did not know what to do nor what to say. I was nine years old and I had never experienced death. My mother was mourning the loss of her father. I had lost a grandfather who I had never met. All I could do was watch.

My mother wanted to replace her old laptop. She wanted to get the right thing so she did a lot of research. She looked at the magazine Consumer Reports to get advice. She wanted to get the correct machine for her needs but she also wanted to get a bargain. She had my sister drive her to various computer stores multiple times. She interrogated the people working in the shops. They had a lot of information and she had only a small bit of information but she was not really interested to get their advice as she felt certain that she knew what she was looking for. My sister and I both suggested that she get a tablet rather than a laptop. She ignored us. Eventually she found something for the price she wanted to spend. It was a laptop designed for children and it had some built-in controls regarding internet use. As a result of this bargain my mother is not able to use many things, including Skype. Since her purchases she has asked various people to set her up with the Skype but eventually we all understood that she would never be able to Skype. She blames the internet for this. She does not acknowledge nor recognise the fact that her computer is self-limiting.

In the early days of the pandemic, my sister arranged a video call with my mother. She telephoned me at a specific time when she was visiting. My mother was delighted to view me over my sister's telephone. She commented on my hair which had grown longer in the lockdown. After about ten minutes, I asked her why she had closed her eyes. She told me that she always closes her eyes when she speaks on the telephone. She says it helps her to concentrate on the person with whom she is conversing. My sister and I have since agreed that my mother has no use for video phone calls.

Working on the obituary together has been a good way to talk about things. I have learned a lot about my mother while we are discussing what should or should not be included. I ask questions and she goes into a lot of detail or else she goes sideways into a tangent that has nothing to do with what we are writing together but it is something that she takes pleasure in explaining. It is not necessarily the detail that we need for the job at hand but it is all part of the larger story that is her life. And these are the things that she chooses to tell in the way that she chooses to tell them.

Mary Stoane died suddenly. It was a brain haemorrhage. She was fifteen years old. Mary Stoane was an only child. Her parents were broken-hearted. The Stoanes were a well-off couple. Spending money on their daughter had been their greatest pleasure. Now they remained well-to-do but they had no Mary to plan and provide for. In the first summer after her death, Mrs. Stoane invited four of Mary's school friends to be her guests on a holiday. It was a way for her to pretend that Mary and her friends were all together and sharing a special treat in Cornwall. The next year she did it again.

Every year for six years, Mrs. Stoane took the four school friends for a holiday in August. Mr. Stoane never joined Mrs. Stoane and the girls on these holidays. He stayed in London with his books. The memories they built together over the years were all contingent on pretending that Mary had been an active participant in each adventure. There were swims in the sea, and favourite teas and memorable cliff walks to discuss and remember. With every passing year it became easier for Mrs. Stoane to believe that Mary had indeed been a part of all of these memories and that she had participated in each holiday excursion. My mother was one of the four girls and she was as eager as the others to play her role in Remembering Mary. Things became more difficult as they got older. It did not feel quite honest to quibble over a pronouncement that Mary preferred custard to tapioca. It did not feel right to say how much Mary loved indoor card games and hot cocoa on a rainy afternoon. And it became increasingly difficult for the four friends to remain as giggly and girlish as they had been at the age of fifteen.

Mrs. Stoane planned the last holiday as a special treat. It was not intended to be the last holiday but that is how things happened. They travelled to Stresa on the Italian coast. The four friends were now four young women. They were twenty-one or twenty-two and they were thrilled to find themselves in Italy. Italian men flirted with them and they were delighted to flirt back. They were happy to be smoking cigarettes and drinking wine and sipping tiny cups of strong black coffee. They had no desire to pretend that they were fifteen and foolish. They were eager to embrace this opportunity to experiment with being glamorous and desirable. Mrs. Stoane did not want them to be desirable. She wanted them to be fifteen-year-old girls. The holiday was a disaster. Mrs Stoane was hurt but the girls were no longer girls. My mother emigrated to New York shortly after this final trip and she never heard from Mrs. Stoane again. One of the school friends later wrote and told her that a public swimming pool had been built in Mary's name.

She loves pens and pencils. She never visits the bank without taking a free pen. The house is full of free pens.

I do not know when she began her preparation for old age. She started by refusing to buy a new dress if it had a zipper up the back. She loved high heels and she had great legs but at some moment she decided that she owned enough pairs of high heels and there was no need to ever buy any more high heels. Practical and simple flat shoes became a preferable option. Then she progressed to fewer buttons. Her hatred of buttons has been going on for a long time. She declared a preference for zippers. She started planning to get old. It was not exactly planning to get old, rather that she was expecting it as an inevitable stage of life. By being ready to be less able, she was preparing. The last thing my mother ever wants to be is helpless, so she needed to think these things through in order to continue to retain her independence.

We speak on the telephone at least once a week. She no longer rings me. She has a service on her telephone that allows her to ring anywhere in the continental United States for free. International calls remain expensive. She finds it annoying that she might ring me and get the answer phone. She hates to pay for herself to talk to a machine. She also despairs that my life is not regular enough. I do not have a normal job with fixed and predictable hours. Along with the five-hour time difference she never knows where I might be nor when. This is not a problem for me. This is my life. But it is a problem for her. I do the calling and I pay for the telephone calls and this is the way that she prefers things to be.

My mother moved to New York City in 1948. Two of her brothers were already there and they invited her to move into their apartment with them while she got herself established in the city. She had four different jobs in the first year. The first job was in the bursar's office at New York University but she was not good at office work and she was bored, so she got a job selling the Encyclopædia Britannica door to door. She loved to talk and she enjoyed calling up her school-girl theatrical experience to assume the role of the book saleswoman. Because of her English accent, people were happy to speak with her. She asked a great many questions and enjoyed learning about the different ways and habits of Americans. She returned home each evening to tell her brothers about the details of American life as she learned them. An early surprise was learning that Americans washed their own windows. She felt certain that even the poorest people in London hired a window cleaner to wash their windows. And if they were too poor to pay a window cleaner, then they just lived with dirty windows, but she swore that she had known no one who would ever consider washing their own windows. Her career as a door-to-door saleswoman did not last long. She had many conversations but she sold few encyclopaedias. Her third job was another sort of office work, this time for a publisher of spiritual texts. Her employers did not feel she had sufficient feeling for the material at hand. Her boredom showed. This job did not last long.

My mother was part of a generation of women who trained as teachers in England during the end of World War II. The country was suffering from a dearth of schoolteachers because so many men and women had gone to war and a lot of them did not return. Teacher training colleges began accelerated courses so that more teachers could be trained quickly to fill the necessary posts. During her first year in New York my mother had been hoping to find a teaching position but because she did not have the necessary qualifications for New York State it was not easy for her to find a job. She was able to get around the state requirements when she was hired to teach at the United Nations School. She taught the children of the serving diplomats so her classroom was full of children from all over the world.

She had applied to work at the United Nations because she adored everything that it stood for.

Our family was the only family I knew that celebrated United Nations Day on the 24th of October. There was a special centrepiece on the dining room table with a tiny flag for every country. This centrepiece appeared every year. My mother baked a cake and the cake had more little flags on it. There might not have been the exact same number of flags on the cake as there were on the centrepiece but the 24th of October was a flag-filled event at our house. We were celebrating the 1945 Charter and the world my mother wanted for us to live in with pride and appreciation. She was determined that we never forget that the United Nations was established to promote and preserve the ideals of world peace and non-violence. She did not want us to assume that living in a democracy and having personal freedoms was something that we should ever take for granted. Conversation at the dinner table on the 24th of October was directed to those issues and world problems currently being discussed at the United Nations. It was not an evening for us to talk about ourselves.

Certain superstitions have remained constant. If any one of us leaves the house to go somewhere and then that person has to come back into the house for some reason, it is imperative that he or she sit down before taking off again. It is only necessary to sit for a second, but still, that person must touch their bottom onto a chair in order to avoid bad luck. My mother always forgets something. The forgetting is getting worse with age. She always needs to go back into the house. It is becoming harder to do that sitting down and getting up thing when ideally she wants to be saving the energy for wherever it is she is going.

My mother was born on the 2nd of February. She enjoys the repetition of the number two in her birthdate and she uses the information as a subtle way to let people know that she is from Somewhere Else. I watched her in the hospital over the course of a day. Each time a nurse or a technician approached her bed, she was asked for her date of birth in order to verify that she was who they believed her to be. Each time she said 2-2-26. Without a pause, she then launched into a brief explanation of how very convenient this date is for her to remember because she is English and in England and indeed in all of Europe the day is listed first and the month follows whereas in the United States it is the other way round so the month is first and the day is second, but luckily she did not have to make any adjustment when she came to live in the United States because the date of her birth works both ways. She is always eager to share this information even with people who do not care at all about how dates are written in England but sometimes they are a tiny bit interested in the fact that she came from England. If they are interested in England at all, it is because that person is a fan of the royal family, or because they have a cousin who went to London once or perhaps they have the dream to visit someday themselves. Whatever spark of interest they show, my mother will jump on it and begin a conversation.

My mother never learned to drive so she has always been dependent on other people to get her to places beyond the short distances she could cover on her bicycle. There is no public transport in the small rural town where we grew up. Since my father's death, she has been obliged to ask various people for lifts when she wants to go anywhere at all. She tries to spread the driving requests around between different friends, as she does not want to abuse the generosity of any single person. Over the years she has developed a kind of system for who to ask to take her where. She does not want a male friend to drive her to the gynaecologist, nor to the urologist. A man is fine to drive her to the dentist or to the foot doctor or even to the Romanian neck doctor. A man is wonderful for taking her to the supermarket. A woman friend is needed to drive her to the gynaecologist because she might want to discuss the appointment afterwards and she feels that she cannot do that with a man.

When I am visiting for a few weeks I become her driver. I take her everywhere. She gets used to me being at her beck and call so she begins to make random and spontaneous requests to stop here for this and there for something else. She invents journeys and visits that are further away from her normal errands and destinations. It is something we can do together.

One afternoon I was driving somewhere. We had a destination. We were discussing various houses and farms as we drove past them. We knew who lived in a lot of the places but a lot of things had changed with time. Some people had died or the families had sold up and moved away. Some houses had burned to the ground. We no longer knew every single person in every single house. Out of the blue, my mother began to rage at me about how foolish people are to seek their ancestors. She said that she had despaired of this obsession during her days as the town librarian. Officially being the librarian was a part-time job. The library was open five afternoons a week. On Monday and Thursday evenings the library was open for two hours. It was also open on Saturday morning. It was a part-time job but it took up the whole week. My mother was required to take courses after she took on the library job. She took the courses required by the State Library in order to prepare herself for the job that she already had. My mother was scornful of those summer visitors who came searching for their family history. She disliked being the one to have to help them. She felt strongly that people should be looking forward not backwards. She thinks it is enough to keep track of your own immediate family without digging for details from the far past.

It was imperative that as small children we learned to carry a pair of scissors correctly.

We ate our evening meal in the dining room. In the winter months when darkness fell early, we always ate by candlelight. There was a lot of ritual about dinner time. It was the time set aside for us all five to sit down together and talk. It was not really about food. My mother is not a good cook. She has never been a good cook. She is not interested in food and the preparation of it nor is she particularly interested in eating. She frequently reminds us that she eats to stay alive, she does not live to eat. She is confused by people who are too interested in food. For her food is fuel. The real reason for sitting around a table is about being together to talk and discuss both our separate activities and the activities of the world. What my mother loves about mealtimes is conviviality. The eating of food is incidental. Food is the fuel that feeds conviviality. It has to be done and it is what brings us together, but because as a family we all ate rapidly, the eating part of dinner was over fast. Often food was cold before it even got to the table anyway because the kitchen was two rooms away and our house was an old cold house. Carrying plates of food from room to room did nothing to help retain the heat. After the eating was over, we talked. The eating part of dinner time was short and the talking part was long. If the telephone rang while we were at the table whoever went to answer it told the caller that one of us would return their call after dinner. Dinner was never interrupted by a phone call and we never left the table until my mother gave us permission to leave the table and then we all left at the same time. Before we left the table, we folded and rolled our napkins and slipped them into silver napkin rings. The napkins were stored in the top drawer of the marble-topped chest, just to the left of the placemats. My parents had heavy napkin rings with their initials engraved on them. My sisters and I had old napkin rings that had once belonged to someone else in the family. Ours were heavy too and the silver was always brightly polished. My napkin ring had the name Willie engraved on it.

My mother has given up feeding the birds. This was the first announcement in today's telephone call. The grey squirrels are always climbing on to the feeders and stealing the birdseed. It does not matter how carefully she hangs the feeders. The squirrels dangle upside down and get at the nuts and the seeds. She bangs on the window to scare them away but they are back again in no time at all. She is annoyed with the squirrels and now she is annoyed with the birds. The birds make too much mess and anyway it all costs too much. She says that the only thing she will miss is the cardinals. They are the most exciting visitors to the feeders. She loves their bright red colour in the winter months but she has decided that a few cardinals are no longer worth the mess and the expense and the anger. She told me that she has seen enough cardinals for one lifetime.

For several years, I attended Girl Scout camp in Vermont. I always received mail on the first day. I was the only girl to get a letter on the first day of camp. Getting a letter on the first full day of camp meant that my mother had posted a little newsy note to me before I even left home. She wrote me a letter before I left home which meant that she had to write carefully so that she was not writing to me about something that I already knew. She always managed to write me something new even though I had been somewhere in the same house when she wrote the letter. She wanted me to know that I was loved and that I was missed.

My mother's brother served in the Royal Air Force during World War II. He was stationed in the Far East. Vera Lynn came to perform for the troops. He saw Vera backstage while she was taking a few minutes of quiet time before she went on stage. She was knitting. He was disappointed to see the gorgeous Vera Lynn doing something so mundane. He was disappointed and he was disgusted. It nearly killed him to see her like that. My mother claims that he never got over it. All of her glamour seeped away. My mother never hears Vera Lynn mentioned without recounting this story. The name Vera Lynn does not come up often in New Hampshire so she does not get many chances to tell the story. Increasingly, people do not even know who Vera Lynn is. Telling the story is a way for my mother to remember her brother and it is a way to feel a little closer to the time and the legacy of Vera Lynn. It is also a way for her to remind people that she grew up Somewhere Else.

There is a container on the top of the stove. It looks like a small metal rubbish bin. Today there are six screwdrivers, a pair of scissors, and a variety of pens and pencils in the container. The objects inside the cylindrical bin vary but this bin is always sitting on the stove, between the two back burners. There used to be a different sort of container but there has always been some form of container holding useful things in a prominent location on my mother's electric stoves over the years. These are things that my mother knows are always helpful to have around in the kitchen and she does not want to have to go looking for them when she needs them. These tools appear to have nothing to do with cooking. Yesterday she decided we should have grilled cheese and tomato sandwiches for lunch. She pulled out two aluminium pie plates and placed them on top of the sandwiches. The can full of screwdrivers and pens was put on top of the aluminium pans in order to squish the bread down. By applying weight to the top of the sandwich while it was heating up in the frying pan, the sandwich became a solid thing with the melted cheese holding everything firmly stuck together. It is the first time I have observed the container doing a job that is not just the job of holding pens and pencils.

A big blizzard is coming. Three days of heavy snow are forecast. I telephoned to ask my mother if she is ready for it. Everyone on the whole east coast of America is expecting to be trapped at home. A friend was going to the supermarket so he telephoned and asked my mother if she needed anything. She asked him to buy her two large onions. Which he did. When she went to put them away, she noticed that she had plenty of carrots. She thought how nice it would be to have a beef stew, but she really did not have any of the ingredients she needed except for the onions and the carrots. Another friend rang to see if there was anything that she could pick up locally for my mother before the storm. My mother put in a request for stewing beef and potatoes. They were delivered and now there is a beef stew simmering in the crock pot. She would not be having beef stew if it were not for the storm and she would not have thought of it if friends had not made the offers of delivering things to her. With plenty of reading material on hand, my mother tells me that she feels ready for the storm. She is now looking forward to being trapped with her stew and her books.

The writing and rewriting of the obituary continues. My mother maintains a file in her file cabinet for the job. One sub-section of the file is dedicated to obituaries of complete strangers that she reads and she likes for some reason. What she likes about a piece is noted on a Post-it note. Sometimes she knows exactly what it is that makes this life so well-written and so interesting but she also cuts out and saves the ones that are dreadful, or those that are funny. She may not want her own obituary to be like these examples but they make her pay attention and she wants to know what makes a reader pay attention to the recording of one life over another. She enjoys a good long read about a person. She loves to recognise what it is that is considered important in the summing-up of a life. My mother enjoys the long obituaries written about famous or influential people that she devours in the New York Times. Family members presenting a piece about their not-famous relative hold a different kind of intimate and personal interest for her. She loves long detailed portraits, but then some days she will have a conversation with someone who says how much they dislike these long obituaries that go on and on and tell so much too much about a life. After that kind of conversation she returns to her own obituary and looks long and hard at it and thinks that perhaps she needs to rethink it. Perhaps she needs to abbreviate it. She worries that maybe it is already too long. She does not want to bore people. She wants them to be interested enough in what is written in her obituary that they will want to read the whole thing. She wants the obituary to be both interesting and unique. She might well do a harsh edit of herself today but a severe cut like this will not last long. She is bound to return to another version as there is a great deal that she feels needs to be said.

My mother reported to me that a neighbour who lives up the road has just bought an assault rifle. He was terrified that Hillary Clinton was going to be elected and that the first thing she would do is that she would stop people from buying guns. So this man went out and bought this gun on election day. He and his lady friend fight a lot. He claims that she gets violent. The man already owns a shotgun and several handguns, none of which make my mother happy. The results of the 2016 election have been shocking enough but an assault rifle across the street outraged her.

As children, we were not allowed to have toy guns. We did not have cap guns nor water pistols. We had no guns of any kind. We did not have guns as children and my parents did not own guns. We were not a very typical family in rural New Hampshire. Gun ownership for hunting and shooting was all normal activity for men and for some women, as was trapping and fishing, but not in our house. In addition to the ban on toy guns we were not given toys that made a lot of noise. If we used something to make noise that was one thing, but toys that were designed to screech or hoot or bang were never welcome. My mother felt she had a right to call limits on things that she herself disliked.

My mother has never acquired a New Hampshire accent. People attribute her way of speaking as an English accent. I do not think she has an English accent any longer. My mother speaks clearly and she has a broad and precise vocabulary. She is eloquent and she enunciates well. People confuse this clarity in her speech with being British. Or people are just confused because she does not sound like everyone else. A new family moved to our town when I was in high school. One of the daughters was in my French class. When our names were called out one morning, the new girl turned to me and asked if my mother was that lady in the library: The One Who Speaks Broken English.

My mother once prepared a tuna casserole that the cat started to eat a few minutes before she was ready to serve it. She quickly covered the top of the casserole with crunched-up potato chips so that no one would notice the cat damage. We ate it. We liked it. We liked it very much. We had guests for supper that night and the guests liked it too. They liked it very much. She told us about the cat after we were finished eating and after the guests had gone home. It was a very Good Housekeeping kind of solution to a very Good Housekeeping kind of problem. From then on, that tuna casserole was always topped with smashed and crumbled potato chips. As a family, we called this Sam's Casserole because Sam was the cat who inspired the change in the recipe.

A kind of panic sets in on a morning that is the first day of the month. My mother has a lot of calendars and she is obliged to change every one of them on the first. She is not happy if the page turning is left to another day. She cannot turn a page on the day before the first day of the month and she is distressed to leave the changing until the second day of the month. She is obsessed by the marking of time. She has calendars upstairs in rooms that she rarely visits. These pages need to be turned. She asks herself why an elderly woman needs so many calendars. She asks this of herself out loud and she frequently asks it of me over the telephone.

My mother wept when Adlai Stevenson died in 1965.

Doing jigsaw puzzles was something we liked to do together. It was a way to talk about various things either in the past or in the present while doing something like looking for the next right piece. A favourite puzzle was a street map of London. It was right out of the A-Z. She liked talking about the streets and the neighbourhoods and recounting things that happened there and there and there. Jigsaw puzzles are no longer an option for my mother as her neck has been giving her so much trouble and the constant act of looking down makes her dizzy. We no longer do jigsaw puzzles together but we do play Scrabble. We never play Scrabble without taking on assumed names. We never play the game as who we are. If I choose to be Harriet, my mother will jump in to be Sybil. My sister, if with us, will then be Lillian. Without planning it, we will have taken on the names of three schoolteachers who occupied their positions in the elementary school for years and years. The person who chooses the first name sort of sets up the possibility for the next two names. Sometimes the names we choose have no connection to anyone. A new name is part of the game. An assumed name gives us the freedom to be ruthless or even the chance to cheat if we feel like trying to slip a word past each other. It is best when my sister joins us. The dynamics of the conversation in and around the game are so much better when we are three.

Bud Thompson is an increasingly regular topic of our telephone conversations. My mother worries about Bud. She has been worrying about him for several years. She told me today that He Will Never Be Happy Again. She has no doubt about that.

Last year Bud and his wife moved into a residential care home. The wife has been suffering from Alzheimer's and it was no longer possible for Bud to care for her on his own at home. He is now ninety-nine years old and she is eighty-nine. He did not feel he could let her go into a home alone so he moved them both into a small apartment. He claims that he does not need the care on offer but she needs it, so he will stay there to be together with her.

She rings Bud once a week and she despairs at the sound of defeat in his voice. Each time I talk to my mother, I listen to her worrying about Bud and in the course of every phone call she tells me more about his life before he got to this sad place. She needs to talk about him because she needs for his life not to evaporate.

She tells me that Bud Thompson was a Troubadour. He started life in Iowa, or Ohio, and from an early age, he travelled the country collecting folk songs. He sang songs and he recorded and wrote down as many songs and tunes as he could learn from other people. By the time he discovered the Shakers, he was already well-known as an expert in the field of folk music. He came to the Shakers because of their singing. In Canterbury, New Hampshire, he stayed for a while and soon became an invaluable part of the community. There were no men left in the village. All of the men were gone. Some of them had died and some had chosen to move out into the world where they did not have to live a life of celibacy. The Shaker way had been to live a celibate life. There was no marriage and there was no sex so there were no offspring. Historically, the solution had been that the Shakers raised all of the orphans for the state of New Hampshire. At the age of eighteen, each orphan had a choice to stay or to go out and make their way in the world. When the state took back the duty of care to raise orphans, the Shakers no longer had children to educate into their way of life. As the only man in a community of ageing Shaker sisters, Bud Thompson helped out where he could although he himself never became a Shaker. He had a wife and together they raised two sons while living in the village. Eventually, he took on the job of director of the community. The Shakers had always been interested in progress and they were always outward looking. Bud became the liaison between the outside world and the community. He was happy to organise tours and to assist in the selling of brooms, seeds, furniture and the crafts that represented Shaker life to people from away. These sales were the way the community stayed viable and visible and the way that they continued to earn money.

Every summer my father gave tours of the village and my mother worked with the herb production volunteers. Bud Thompson took to calling these women The Strippers because they seemed to be endlessly stripping dried herbs off their stalks to make sachets and other things to sell in the Shaker shop.

Bud Thompson is a living encyclopaedia of Shaker knowledge. My mother despairs that his knowledge is going to disappear when he dies. When the board decided to take the community into the world in a more commercial way, Bud stepped down and left them to it. His knowledge became redundant. The business-people now in charge felt that they knew plenty. These people had marketing degrees, and fundraising skills and they knew how to make money from busloads of tourists from out of state.

Bud and his wife moved away from the village and went to establish the Museum of American Indians in Warner. All the while Bud continued to collect folk music.

Now he is trapped in an old people's home with his wife who does not remember who he is. My mother repeats that He Will Never Be Happy Again. Bud Thompson is a part of our every conversation.

A list like this is not sufficient to illustrate my mother's life in any coherent way. Even while I am looking for them, I cannot find all of the pieces that make up the whole. I can only remember what I remember. Forgetting seems to be as big a part of the exercise as the remembering.

Eight Affections
- Puns
- English poetry of the First World War
- Buying a box of chocolates for herself and having it gift-wrapped
- Roman numerals.
- Addresses written in lower case. Anything written in lower case.
- Collective nouns
- Rotating the mugs in a particular order so that she uses a new one every day of the week
- Crossword puzzles

In the last four years, every time we speak on the telephone, my mother reports to me exactly how many days Donald Trump has left in his term as President. She has a digital calendar counting down the days. This calendar sits beside the back door. It is not a calendar that she needs to change herself. It is set for the four years of his term. It computes the countdown by itself every single day. She is obsessed with getting him out of office. She claims that even though she is old, she feels that she cannot die while That Man is in the White House. Each phone call involves a certain amount of time remarking or grumbling about his comments or his behaviour. She tries not to say his name out loud. After five or ten minutes of despairing, she calls a halt to this line of conversation and says that we should not waste our telephone time on That Man.

The house is full of clocks. My mother likes clocks. We often received clocks as gifts. In my mother's opinion there is nothing nicer that she can give us. Except a book. Every clock in the house runs at a different time. The separate clocks with their different times are consistent. The two clocks in the bedroom are both set to be twenty minutes fast. They are always twenty minutes fast. All of the other clocks in the house are five minutes fast. Except for the kitchen clock. The kitchen clock is always ten minutes fast. There has always been a clock over the refrigerator and it has always been ten minutes fast. There used to be a red clock in the shape of an apple over the refrigerator. The red apple clock belonged to a great aunt and for some reason that clock came to us after she died. I do not think anyone really liked it but it was the clock that was there so we lived with it for as long as it lasted. We spoke of it as Aunt Vic's Clock if we spoke of it at all. It was never referred to as the Apple Clock. Aunt Vic's Clock was replaced at some point with an unpleasant thing that had forks and spoons sticking out in all directions. My mother claimed to like it because it had Roman Numerals. She has a particular fondness for clocks with Roman Numerals. No one else liked this clock. I was pleased when I returned for a visit and found that it had been replaced. When the new plain white circular clock was hung above the refrigerator, it was set to retain the same ten minutes of extra time that the kitchen clock has always had. It has always been ten minutes fast. At the age of ninety-one, my mother still knows each clock by its fastness or slowness and it is always reset to stay exactly that way.

These are the things that we know to be constants. So long as my mother's house is my mother's house we expect these things to remain the same.

My mother became an American citizen in 1975. She has not felt the need to list this detail in the obituary, or not yet anyway. Because New Hampshire is where the first Presidential primaries have traditionally been held, my mother shook hands with a large number of Presidential hopefuls. It was not that she went looking for them. They came to our town and walked around shaking hands with people. It is a very small town. There are not many people out and about on a weekday morning. My mother was one of the few people always out on foot rather than in a car so she was an available hand to be shaken. She never mentioned to the hopefuls that she did not have a vote. She had strong opinions on politics and finally wearied of not being able to have her say at the ballot box. In applying for citizenship, she was obliged to study the United States Constitution and to attend a morning in court where the Judge directed questions at the individual applicants. She had studied hard and was disappointed that the Judge did not ask more of her newly acquired information.

Every knife in my mother's kitchen is dull. The dullness makes cutting things difficult and dangerous but my mother will not hear any arguments. She feels that she is safer with dull knives and nothing we say can change her mind.

As my mother has grown older it has been increasingly difficult to find the right gift to send for her birthday and at Christmas. At a certain point, I got into the habit of buying a gift certificate for her favourite bookshop. I purchased a certificate for the age she was about to celebrate. At age eighty-nine she received $89.00. At age ninety-three, she received $93.00. The people from the bookshop were always encouraging me to round off the number to a tidy amount, but I never did that. It would have ruined the pleasure that my mother took in getting the gift certificate. I ask the people in the shop to choose an attractive card, but not a cute card, and to post the certificate inside the card for my mother to receive in time for her birthday. My mother has no interest in anything cute. Receiving the gift certificate was one thing and then choosing the right person to drive her to the bookshop and letting her peruse for an hour or so was another thing. The amount of the gift does not really matter because it is free money. The free money offers her the freedom to buy whatever she feels like buying and whatever she wants to buy on that day. The books or cards or calendars that she chooses to purchase with her gift certificate are actual gifts. As well as having boxes and boxes of note cards under her desk available for any event, my mother loves to buy greetings cards. She spends a long time standing and looking and carefully choosing what might be appropriate for this person or that person. The standing up is the most difficult thing about being in the bookshop. When I am sent a card that my mother considers an extremely beautiful card, she writes the greeting and includes her love to me on a Post-it note inside the card. This is never discussed but I know that her intention is that I will be able to use this card again for someone else. The fact that she does not sully the card with her own handwriting is a sign that she considers the card just too good for one outing.

My mother has taken to reading the sports pages in recent years as sports are a topic of conversation for a lot of people. Sports are not as problematic as politics. Our family has never been interested. Our family has been so uninterested in sports that I was questioned carefully when I wanted to play on teams and to be required to attend endless practices. Heading out to walk through the woods on snowshoes or on cross-country skis on a bright winter day was also questioned. My mother could never understand why I would want to do something physical when I could stay indoors and read a book. So it is a surprise to find out that my mother is now perusing the sports pages in the local newspaper. When she is being driven to an appointment by her friend who is an enthusiastic fan, she wants to be able to discuss Ice Hockey with him. He loves Ice Hockey and he follows the season with a fervour close to obsession. She herself is not interested in Ice Hockey. I do not think she has ever watched a game but she will follow the scores and the wins and the various players in the newspapers so that she can discuss these things in an informed and interested manner with him. My mother feels that as a passenger in someone else's motor car, she should be a good guest and maintain a conversation about something in which the driver of the car is interested.

We stood in the bank together while she withdrew her money for the month. Not for the first time, she explained to me that she does not use ATM machines and although she will use cheques or credit cards to purchase things, she prefers to do most transactions with cash. She said everything in a loud voice. She said everything in a louder voice than necessary. I was standing right beside her. The bank teller was the only other person in the room and the room was not large. My mother announced in her loud clear voice that she kept her cash for the month, as well as a little extra for emergencies, in the freezer because she felt it was a safe place. The teller looked at me and she raised one eyebrow. My mother continued to speak emphatically about how she is careful who she tells this to as she would not like the money to be stolen. My mother needs hearing aids but she refuses to buy them. She says everyone she knows who has bought hearing aids considers them a waste of money. She is going to buy a new refrigerator instead.

As a young girl, my mother got her first library card from the Carnegie Library in Stoke Newington. She read voraciously. She read everything she could. For some reason at that time, they kept novels away from young people. As a reader she was allowed one volume of fiction and six non-fiction books at any given time. Library bindings had only the author name and the Dewey Decimal number showing on the spine. She rarely knew what she was getting but just worked her way along the shelves alphabetically until she familiarised herself with some names. Poetry and plays fell into the category of non-fiction. She fell in love with poetry. She read poetry and memorised poetry and to this day she can still recite an enormous number of long poems word for word.

My mother has written poetry and published poetry and judged poetry competitions and used her fine calligraphic hand to write out poetry for presentations and for gifts. In recent years she began to experiment with the form of Haiku. She feels its brevity is suited to her older age. The need to be succinct means that there are no superfluous words. Her haiku, largely political or at least topical in subject matter, are regularly published in the state newspaper. She becomes annoyed if she does not have at least one published each week. There are two haiku included in her obituary so far and she is considering a third: one at the beginning, one in the middle and one as an ending.

My mother suffers from insomnia but she does not count sheep to help herself to fall asleep. Instead, on some nights she recites poetry to herself and other nights she amuses herself by singing Broadway musicals because she delights in knowing all of the words of all of the songs.

There are rituals that I have never understood. After washing the dishes, my mother boils a kettle of water and pours the boiling water over the silverware. The silver is then dried with a tea towel and tossed down on the counter in a messy sprawl where it lays for several hours or days until it reaches the state that my mother considers to be thoroughly dry. Then it is gathered up and put away.

My little sister and I were separated at nap time because there was always a strong possibility that if we remained in the same room, we would not sleep. We would find something else to do. Naps were not the way we wanted to spend our time together. If my mother put us onto different beds in different rooms, there was a better chance of each of us going to sleep. One afternoon I was on my parents' bed and I was bored. I was not sleepy and I was not sleeping. I did not have my sister there to distract me. I do not know how old I was but I was old enough to know how to write. I was old enough to know my letters but I was young enough to need a nap. I picked up a nail file and began to carve the word Mummy on the headboard of the bed. I inscribed Mummy in large capital letters on the side of the bed where my mother always slept. I was just stating the obvious. We all knew which side of the bed she slept on. I was identifying her assigned place.

My mother came into the bedroom just as I finished writing her name. She was furious. I had scratched large letters right through the varnish and into the wood. The nail file was a strong and efficient tool for the job. The first M was about three inches tall. After the first letter, the others were unevenly sized. My mother was angry and I was annoyed. She had interrupted me before I had time to write Daddy on the other side of the headboard.

Tonight I am sleeping in that same bed in what was once their bedroom. Four years ago, they moved their sleeping downstairs into what was the living room. They bought a new bed and they left the old bed upstairs. Sleeping on the ground floor made it easier for them to walk to the bathroom at night without having to go up and down the steep staircase. It was a good idea at the time and it quickly became a better idea as my father's health and strength deteriorated. It was many decades ago when I carved Mummy into this headboard. Several years passed before it got repaired. I admired my big letters whenever I saw them but now they are gone. The headboard has been sanded down and refinished. There is no sign of my handiwork. There is the slightest sort of soft dip in the wood where the sanding had to go deep to erase the word, but no one would notice that unless they knew to look for it.

Beside this bed there is a blue container with pens and pencils and bookmarks in it. There are thirty-four bookmarks in this cup. One of them is made of thin wood. My mother has more bookmarks than anyone I know. I just found sixteen more held together with a thick blue rubber band.

The cheese grater is kept in a low cupboard. It is on the bottom shelf of the cupboard and it is pushed all the way to the back behind heavy saucepans and mixers and other things that are rarely required. The grater is in a difficult place to reach. This is intentional. The grater is one of those four-sided stainless steel cheese graters that stands up by itself and has a handle at the top. My mother keeps it in a clear plastic bag with a twisty-tie closing it. The grater is old and the last time I saw it, there was a little rust on the cutting edges. When asked why she keeps it in such an inaccessible place, my mother defends the placement by saying that she does not like the grater. She does not like the grater and she does not want to use it. She is frightened of the grater because she feels it would be terribly easy to scrape the skin off her knuckles when using it. By keeping it in a difficult place she makes it impossible to reach and therefore she has an excuse for not using it.

I made some notecards for my mother and sent them off to her as a gift. She loves new notecards. She has many boxes of them piled up under her desk. She writes a lot of notes to people. She writes notes for birthdays, for sympathy, for congratulations and of course to say thank you. My mother is adamant that a thank-you note must always be written on paper. She has grown fond of using e-mail in recent years but she does not believe that an e-mail is the proper and correct way to say thank you to anyone for anything. She likes to have the right notecard for the right occasion and for the right person. Within each box of notes, there is a list of who she has sent that card to. It is important to her that she not send the same card to a person twice. At any given moment, my mother will have a minimum of thirty different boxes of cards in the teetering piles underneath her desk. She is always buying new boxes of cards. It is very nearly her favourite thing about being taken to a museum or a galley. She is excited and stimulated to get to an exhibition, not least of all because that in itself is a rare event, but she would never feel the trip to be complete if she did not have a good long time in the gift shop choosing at least one new box of notecards.

In making the cards to send to her, I chose flowers from my selection of dried vegetation and I glued one blossom onto each of the heavy folded cards. I secured each stem with two very thin and delicate strips of brown tape. After I sent the cards off in the post, I acknowledged to myself that I was more than a little bit worried that my mother will not really like these cards with the brown tape and that she will feel that they are perhaps not refined enough. She might think them a little bit rough looking. What I know that she will like is the heavy creamy paper of each card. She will love the fine thick envelopes which accompany each card. If she does not like the cards very much she will use them rarely and she will convince herself that she is saving them for someone special. There is a good chance she will use the cards to write notes of thanks to me. By sending my own cards back to me, she will be proving to me that she is using them.

My mother's bread bin is full of empty plastic bags. Bread is not kept in the bread bin. Bread is kept in the freezer.

I have a photograph of my mother posing as a dead person. She was in the hospital after having a small stroke. She was convinced that she was fine and that no lasting damage had been done by the little stroke but the medical team insisted that she stay in the hospital overnight and that she receive a barrage of tests before being sent home. I was sitting beside her bed when she told me that she was pleased not to be dead yet. She asked me how I thought she would look as a corpse. She crossed her arms over her chest with her hands flat and directed up toward her shoulders and turned her head to the side. Her eyes were open and looking imp- ishly skyward. Her mouth was in a small smile. It was not a smile that suggested serenity. It was a smile that meant there was a joke and she was part of the joke. She insisted that I take a photograph so that she could get an idea of how she will look when the time comes. Before I took the photograph she applied some lipstick.

Eyeglasses are always placed on a surface with the lens side facing down and the stems sticking straight up in the air. This means the glasses will get caught by the passing movement of an arm or a sleeve and they will be knocked to the floor. It also guarantees that the lenses will be scratched.

For many years I thought my mother wanted me to know more about her family and her past. I thought that she felt I was not interested enough. Now I understand that she does indeed want me to know about her family but she only wants me to know those things that she chooses to tell me. She is not really wanting me to dig too deeply. She and her four brothers and a small amount about her parents is plenty. She is telling me the things she thinks are important for me to know. She is leaving out a lot.

Sometimes my mother's family had money and they had a maid. Sometimes there was no money and no maid. Sometimes they lived in apartments where they were offered six months' free rent but they would stay for a year or eighteen months without paying any rent and then suddenly they would be forced to move out quickly. Sometimes they had to move in the middle of the night. When there was no money and times were precarious there was also little food. My mother told us how special and rare it was to have scrambled eggs during the war when eggs were not always readily available. Other times she recounts how horrible it was that her mother served her runny scrambled eggs for her birthday tea because there was nothing else in the house to eat and she was supposed to consider herself lucky to have anything at all.

Two places that my mother never mentions when recounting London locations are Pentonville Prison and Wormwood Scrubs. Her father spent time in both of these prisons. He was not very good at making money and supporting his family. There were various projects and schemes over the years. Most of them were not successful. A sister-in-law invited my grandfather to participate in a venture smuggling watches out of Switzerland and into England. He was the one who was caught.

At some point in their growing up, my grandmother changed the names of my mother and her brothers so that they would sound less Jewish and more English. She changed their names so that they would have a better chance to get ahead. She pushed them all to work hard in school and to get good grades. My mother loved to learn and she loved books and she worked hard and enthusiastically and earned herself a scholarship to a good girls' school. My grandmother took full credit for this scholarship and claimed that it was her own brains that my mother had inherited. She claimed that she gave my mother constant encouragement and fed her copious quantities of carrots so that her eyes were good. That is why she was able to study a lot.

One day my mother's mother got angry about something and she tore up my mother's library card. It was the cruellest punishment she could inflict. My mother was heartbroken. Her library card was her most prized possession. She was terrified that she would be unable to replace it.

The small glass bowls stacked in my mother's cup-board have a folded piece of paper towel placed in between each bowl.

My mother has no interest in sewing. She did not make us clothes when we were children, although she could hem up a skirt if necessary. She was a good knitter and she made us many sweaters and mittens over the years. Sewing was something that she avoided. She always preferred to be reading rather than sewing.

The invention of printed iron-on name tapes was great news to her. When we went off to summer camp all of our clothing had to be labelled. Some things, like rain jackets, could be written upon with a special Laundry Pen. A Laundry Pen was special because it was indelible and it did not wash off in the washing machine. The line drawn with a laundry pen was fat like a crayon line so it was not suitable for everything. Tee-shirts, shorts, bathing suits and sweatshirts all needed labelling. Sewing in the small woven tapes with our individual names was a slow and thankless job. If we were going to lose something, surely we would lose it whether or not it was labelled. Sewing in each little tape only involved a few stitches at each end but there were so many of them to be done. I am not sure why she did not set us the task of sewing our own names into our own clothing. When my mother discovered iron-on tapes, it sounded so easy and so modern. The tapes arrived as a long roll and when cut off, each label had straight corners. The corners needed to be rounded off with scissors to ensure that they did not immediately peel off the garment. Cutting corners became a new tedious task.

I no longer receive birthday gifts nor Christmas presents from my mother. There is the difficulty of getting to shops, and then there is the palaver of wrapping the parcels and waiting for someone to drive her to the post office. It is all too much. She finds the price of international postage horrifying. She does want occasions to be celebrated with a gift of some sort, so she writes me a cheque and posts it enclosed inside a carefully chosen and always lovely card. Because my mother does not throw things away and she does not like to waste anything, she writes these cheques on cheques that are left over from old bank accounts. Not wanting to waste anything means that old cheque books are often used as scrap paper or for shopping lists. When she writes a birthday cheque she uses one of the cheques from a defunct account. These cheques look good. They look like legal tender. They look like any cheque that can be taken to the bank and deposited or exchanged for cash. There might be a law against writing cheques on accounts that no longer exist, but that is not a problem. I never take these cheques to the bank. The idea is that my mother will deposit the amount of money described on the cheque into the bank account that I retain in town. I keep a bank account for exactly this sort of thing. Sometimes she remembers to go to the bank and deposit the money and sometimes she forgets.

My mother loves to recount what she considers her Most Magical Moment. She was standing in a friend's rose garden in the dropping darkness of a summer evening. It had gone beyond dusk and it was nearly full night. She and her friend, who was visiting from South Africa, and their hostess stood together in the quiet. One recited the first line and without a pause another one of them recited the second and the third chimed in with the third line.

It is a beauteous evening, calm and free
The holy time is quiet as a Nun
Breathless with adoration

Together they quoted these lines from Wordsworth in the dark and under the stars. She cannot remember who spoke the first line and who spoke the second nor the third but she loves that they did it spontaneously. Unrehearsed and quietly.

I watched my mother washing some blueberries this afternoon. She was doing the job with a lot of concentration so I did not interrupt her to ask why she was doing the things that she was doing. She poured the quart of berries into a large bowl of cool water and left them to float around for a few minutes. The berries were then poured through a sieve. When most of the water had drained off, the blueberries were decanted onto the top of the stove. My first assumption was that she was using the pilot light to dry the berries but then I remembered that the oven and the stove top are electric. There is no pilot light. There is no source of warmth or heat for drying anything. And it is not easy to gather together the rolling berries from the top of the stove when they are considered dry.

When we are on the telephone together my mother often speaks of The Next Envelope. This is meant as a promise but some days it sounds like a threat. She will not post an envelope until she has put enough different things into it. She will not post an envelope until she has enclosed enough different things for it to earn its postage stamp. Articles cut from magazines or from the newspaper, old photographs, and letters received from someone I might know and want to receive the news of. There are articles about exhibitions in New York and Boston and cut-out articles about restaurants and chefs. These things might not be things that she is interested in but they will be things that she thinks that I might be interested so that is enough of a reason to cut out and enclose them. She also removes any unfranked stamps that arrive on my letters. She knows that I will soak the stamps off and re-use them. She often includes stamps from England as well as those from Ireland. She instructs me that I can give the English ones to someone who lives over there.

On Thursday I received an envelope holding twenty-two family photographs. My mother identified a few of the people but said that she did not know who or where or when most of the pictures were taken but she thought I might like to have them anyway. Her mother had written on the back of some of the photographs but what she wrote seems to be consistently unrelated to what was pictured. She wrote MY MAID HAS BIG LEGS on the reverse of a photo which had no maid in it and no legs on view.

16 March 2016
- New York Times piece about crossword puzzles and the use, re-use and logic of crossword words and clues.
- One of her own haikus which was recently published in the Concord Monitor, but this version copied out on the back of a daily tear-off calendar page.
- New York Times article about the Artist Pension Trust
- New York Times article about the designer of the Bialetti coffee maker who died and had his ashes placed in one of the very coffee machines that he had designed.
- Short note written on the back of two pages of a daily tear-off page calendar
- One poem and one cartoon, both cut out from the Concord Monitor.
- Article from The New Yorker with Destination Note for Murray's Cheese Bar on Bleecker Street in NYC

20 January 2020 Padded envelope
- Harry S. Truman calendar. (I have no particular

interest in Harry S. Truman and I do not think my
mother does either. I think she sent me this calendar
because it was just too good to throw away)
- a small Ziploc bag containing dental picks and two
  new heads for the electric toothbrush
- an exquisite tiny silver pickle fork made by my
  father
- a well-worn pair of leather gloves. (My mother
  and I wear a similar size in gloves but this pair are
  neither wanted nor needed. They are too old to be
  useful to anyone.)
- Christmas cards and notes sent to her by people
  who she knows and who I know too forwarded on
  for my interest with a Post-it note saying DO NOT
  RETURN!

14 February 2021
- A birthday card for my birthday with nothing
  written inside it so that I can use it again for
  someone else.
- A tiny Ziploc bag holding 30 melatonin tablets (I
  must have mentioned once that melatonin is not
  available for purchase in Ireland)
- A birthday cheque from a defunct bank account
- A small pad of paper sent to her for free from
  St Joseph's Indian School in South Dakota as a
  Lakota (Sioux) fundraiser
- An unfranked Irish postage stamp, cut off a recent
  envelope

My younger sister and I were left to stay with our Great Aunt Vic for a few days. When we were in the houses of other people, we were quiet and a little bit timid and we became fussy eaters. Aunt Vic had never had children herself so my mother gave her a few suggestions both about bedtimes and about food. With a view toward making mealtimes easier, my mother informed Aunt Vic about a few of our preferred tastes. She mentioned that we loved to nibble raw carrot sticks. The first day, a big bowl of carrot sticks appeared on the lunch table. Aunt Vic had taken my mother's advice to heart and she had cut up eight or ten carrots for us. The leftover carrot sticks were then stored in the refrigerator, held together firmly with a rubber band. These same carrot sticks appeared at every subsequent meal. With each arrival they were a little more dried out. They dried out and as they dried they curled. With each appearance of the tightly banded carrot sticks, we were less interested. We struggled to eat any carrots at all. When my parents returned to collect us, Aunt Vic informed my mother in a huffy voice that she had been given false information. She was angry because she felt that my mother had wasted her time. She informed my mother in no uncertain terms that my sister and I did not like carrot sticks.

For six or seven years each letter that I received from my mother had a line quoted from a Broadway musical written on the back of the envelope. One day she just stopped doing that. There was no reason. It was just time for a change.

There were four brothers, three of whom married and had families and one of them never married. He died at the age of seventy-five. He lived by himself in a one-bedroom apartment. He lived alone and he died alone. It was a week before anyone found him. He had lived quietly. No one noticed him when he was alive so they barely noticed his absence when he was dead. He lived as a recluse but he never intended to be a recluse. It just happened.

He left some orderly papers on the telephone table, so the caretaker of the building knew to ring my mother who lived far away. The caretaker gave her the news.

This brother had trained as an engineer, and he had travelled all over the world for his work. On one trip, he fell in love with a stewardess. It was love at first sight for him. He began to plan as many flights as possible with the same airline, always hoping to meet the stewardess. Her name was Lorna. He dreamed about Lorna and he planned his future with her in it. She knew nothing about these plans.

One day he waited for Lorna in the airport. As the flight crew walked off the plane in a little group he asked if he could speak to her for a minute. The others walked on and she waited, standing up straight with her cheerful stewardess face in place. He spelled out his good prospects in his field and his financial stability and he asked her if she would marry him. She laughed a deep, chuckling laugh and said that of course she would not marry him. She said she would need to be desperate to marry a man like himself. She thanked him for the offer and ran off to catch up with the rest of the crew.

He was disappointed but he told my mother that he was not defeated. He kept track of Lorna over the years. He knew when she married and later, he knew when she was widowed. On retiring from his job after so many years of travel he did not want any more travel. He settled down in the same apartment he had been in and out of for thirty years. Since he had never spent much time there it still looked like the furnished apartment that it was. Everything was brown or beige and everything was devoid of personality.

This brother had no hobbies. He had no hobbies and he had no social life. He was not skilled at occupying himself without the demands of a job, but he slowly found things to amuse him. He liked to listen to the radio. He listened to radio stations from all over the world. He listened to the radio and he sharpened pencils. He had a lot of pencils. He bought himself an electric pencil sharpener and he delighted in perfect points. All of his pencils were lined up on the windowsills with their points pointing outwards. Every windowsill was full of pencils in parallel lines. Not one pencil was touching another pencil. He kept the city telephone books in a tall pile in one corner. He had never thrown one out. He had one for every year since he had been in the apartment. The Yellow Pages were all piled together chronologically at the bottom of the pile. He enjoyed reading through the telephone directory. Names that amused him were underlined with a sharp pencil. Sometimes he would research a name in order to find out how many years that same name was listed. He kept an eye out for when someone moved house. He had time to think about whether the person with that name had died or whether they had moved away. He felt that he was connected to that person. He felt that if he did not worry and care about where the person went then no one else would. He had explained this pastime to my mother during their monthly telephone conversations.

He kept his winter gloves lined up along one wall. They were on the floor with the fingers pointing to the wall, left glove beside right glove with the thumbs touching. When my mother came to clear out the apartment she noted that every single pair of gloves he owned had been given to him as a gift from her.

My mother was the named executor. Expenses were covered for her to travel to her brother's city and to stay in a hotel for as long as was necessary to sort things out. Her brother had told her that he was leaving her everything he had. He had often repeated that so she had no reason to believe otherwise. When the reading of the will was held at the solicitor's office, one million dollars was left to Lorna. My mother was bequeathed five thousand dollars, plus her costs for travel and the job of sorting out the pencils and the telephone directories and the gloves.

The house has two staircases going up to the first floor from the ground floor. Both of the staircases are extremely steep. They are nearly ladder-like in their steepness. The stairs are steep and the steps are narrow. They are not practical stairs for an older person. They are not safe stairs for anyone. My mother uses these staircases for her morning exercise on those winter days when there is too much ice or too much snow and she knows she will not be able to go out for a walk. She goes up one set of stairs and then she comes down the other one. I do not know how many times she does this and I do not know if she always goes up the same set of stairs and down the other, or if she varies her direction and her route. The stairs are one dangerous thing but all of the old wooden floors throughout the house are uneven and rolling. The entire house is full of accidents waiting to happen.

My mother keeps track of how many servings of ice cream she gets from each container that she buys. She always buys the same brand and she always buys vanilla. Friendly's French Vanilla. To keep track of her ice cream portions, she rubs the top of the cardboard tub until it is dry. Then she uses a Sharpie pen to mark down the bowlful she has just scooped out. She uses a hatch mark to note the portion. She told me once that she gets fourteen portions to a container. If she always buys the same ice cream in the same size container and if she is the only one eating it and her portion sizes are the same size portions every time, I do not know why she needs to mark down the serving with her Sharpie every time she has a bowl of ice cream. But she does.

Both Thanksgiving and Christmas were holidays that my mother was obliged to learn. They were not part of her life before she moved to the United States. She took her cues from my father's mother and from friends along the way and over the years, she tailored these holidays to be specific to our family.

At Christmas, it was important to my mother that she always gave us something that she had made for us and she always gave us a book.

My father's sister wrapped her Christmas presents perfectly. Not only was the wrapping paper brand new and unwrinkled, but it was tight and the corners were crisp. The wrapping paper was pulled so firmly into place that my aunt used no tape to close the packages. My sisters and I always marvelled at her fine technique. We were as interested in the fact that the gifts were being wrapped without the use of sticky tape as we were with anything that might be inside the package. We knew that whatever was in the box would be the same gift for all three of us but each one would be a different colour. We spent much more time on the outside of the box and we wondered every year if this aunt had gone to a special class to learn how to wrap her parcels without tape. Her ribbons were also perfect and snug and the bows were perfectly formed. Most of our ribbons were raggedy. They were re-used from year to year so we appreciated the influx of new ribbons and bows. My mother was not at all interested in the tight corners and the immaculate bows. When pressed to admire the technique she never said anything more than to remark that Yes, It Is A Skill.

Every Christmas we received a number of gifts from whatever pets we had at the time. The dog always gave us new socks and the cats gave us underpants. My mother would have been buying these things for us anyway but receiving everyday things wrapped up made them exciting and special. It also made the pile of gifts under the tree a bit bigger. Presents from the animals were always wrapped in awkward newspaper parcels. There were no ribbons on the gifts from the animals, just a name written in clumsy crayon. My mother was firm in her knowledge that cats and dogs could not hold pens so that was why they used crayons. And they certainly could not tie bows.

All of my mother's house plants are decorated at Christmas, even those plants that are off in a spare room that no one ever goes into except to water the plants. The plants that are sitting alone in a window to get any tiny bit of winter sun are decorated just as carefully as those in the more public rooms of the house. There is a box of skewers, the long skinny kind made for making shish kebabs on the barbecue, in with the Christmas things. Tiny red bulbs are balanced on the long sticks that are pushed into the soil in the plant pots.

My mother dislikes strong smells. She has particularly negative feelings about perfumed things. She hates scented soap and scented candles. She is not a fan of flowers with strong scents. If I send flowers to be delivered for a special occasion, they must be the sort with little or no smell. Tulips are good. Lilies are bad.

A dear friend celebrated her 100th birthday and then she died the very next day. Someone collected and drove my mother to the funeral. Now she is bemoaning the fact that the priest did not even know the dead woman and he just spoke generically about her. My mother felt this was a terrible insult to the memory of her friend. On top of that, the incense and the many floral bouquets were too much for her. She is adamant that this is the last funeral she will attend in a Catholic church. It is partly the smells but I think my mother is mostly just tired of attending funerals. There are fewer and fewer people with whom she can share memories and the funerals are never much fun. She has always set great store by her friendships and her ability to have different kinds of friends. She is finding that it is a problem to outlive so many of them.

There was red and white linoleum on the kitchen floor. It was a basket-weave pattern. One morning the cat knocked the iron off the ironing board when my mother was out of the room. By the time she returned to the kitchen there was a solid black burn mark in the exact shape of the iron. We lived with that burn mark in the linoleum for years after that. My mother claimed that she loved it because it reminded her how very much she hated ironing.

My mother steps out onto the back porch every night before she goes to bed. She waits until she is in her nightdress and wearing her dressing gown and slippers and she has washed both her face and her teeth. It does not matter how cold it is. If the snow is drifting and blowing she might slide her feet into a pair of boots. It does not matter if the temperature is well below zero. It is important that she go outdoors to look at the sky and to see the moon if it is in any way visible. She believes it is a healthy habit to take a few big gulps of fresh air before going to sleep.

When we were growing up, there was Butter and then there was Real Butter. Butter was the everyday margarine that came in long sticks as American butter did. Or does. Four sticks to a box. A stick is a quarter pound of butter. Butter is sold in a box and a box of four sticks equals a pound of butter. Butter dishes are designed to accommodate these long sticks. Our butter dish was long and rectangular and it had a cover that fitted over the top without touching the sides of the butter. The cover of our butter dish was made of transparent plastic. Real Butter looked just the same as the margarine that we called butter. Sometimes the Real Butter was a little bit more yellow than the margarine we called butter. That might have been how we knew what it was. The main way that we knew it was Real Butter was because its presence was always announced. Real Butter not Butter. It did not matter if we knew what it was, nor if we could taste the difference, because it always arrived as something special. Real Butter was something to be noticed and noted. It was not for daily life. Real Butter was for guests, and holidays and for corn on the cob. In recent years my mother's Butter, in its long narrow dish, has been stored in her microwave oven. Both winter and summer. My mother prefers her Butter to be at room temperature, never cold from the refrigerator.

My mother has taken to speaking of herself as The Last Pebble on The Beach. All of her brothers have died and she is the last of the siblings alive. She feels that this is both a kind of lonely place to be but that it is also a surprise. She sort of feels that she bears some degree of responsibility to remember her brothers, but since she never expected to be the last of her immediate family, she does not know whether to consider this an obligation or simply a fact. She repeats the expression Last Pebble on The Beach often so I think it is important to her that she is the remaining representative.

Places in the downstairs of the house are defined by pieces of large furniture that have always been present. The Grain Chest. The Apothecary Chest. The Marble-Topped Chest. These are large, handsome and cumbersome pieces with multiple functions and large surface areas. There can never be enough surfaces for the many piles of things. I think that it is important for my mother to see the things that she needs and wants to keep track of. It is not just chairs that have piles of things on them. The Apothecary Chest, with its twenty-eight drawers, has traditionally been the place where all of the books borrowed from the library were stacked. Those books coming into the house and those read and ready to be returned. They all gathered onto one end of the Apothecary Chest. When my parents moved from the house I grew up in to the house where my mother now lives alone the library books changed location. They are now piled up on the Grain Chest but there are no longer the large number of library loans of five separate people. There are only my mother's books. The librarian sends books to my mother every week. Sometimes they have telephone conversations if my mother is seeking a particular title or if she wants to discuss a book she has just read. At other times the librarian selects and sends the books she thinks that my mother might enjoy.

There is a large desk in one corner of the dining room. The desk has always been in the corner of the dining room, both in this house and in the old house. Because my mother is now readying herself for the move to live with my sister, she surprised us by announcing that she dislikes this desk and that she has always disliked this desk. The desk was my father's great love and he had it refinished for her, exposing the light warm colour of the wood. It is a large bureau desk with a sloping front. When opened out the generous writing area rests on two open drawers, but it is officially held open with a chain on each side. The drawers were an extra security for the weight of the wood and the added weight of a writer's arms. The opened-up desk is full of cubby holes and little shelves and drawers. The whole thing stands on long thin legs that remind me of the legs of a greyhound. I have always thought it the most wonderful object. This desk is more of a place than a thing. I have never doubted that my mother loves it as much as I do. I am stunned to find that she does not want this desk to move with her.

In preparing for this move into my sister's house, she has begun to pack even though we have told her that this work can all be done for her. Today on the telephone, she told me that she filled a box with wooden things: Wooden platters. Salad bowls. Nut bowls. Fruit bowls. Cutting boards and wooden implements. All things made of wood. Yesterday she filled a box with measuring things. I wondered as she told me this how many rulers and tape measures she owns. It could not be enough to fill a box. Of course she did not mean rulers and tape measures. She was packing measuring cups and spoons. I wondered if there were enough of these to fill even a small box. And I question why she needs all these measuring things since she has done no baking at all for at least ten years.

My family has had the same telephone number for my entire life. When I was a child we only needed to dial four digits. I do not know when it was increased to seven digits. Now that my mother is about to move, this telephone number will no longer be the number that I can dial without thinking.

My mother has various theories for evading death. One is that she never sits still for more than twenty minutes. After twenty minutes, she jumps up and moves around and then she returns to whatever she was reading or watching or eating. It is distracting to share a table with her. She says old age kills by stiffening and she is determined not to stiffen up. She is convinced that if she keeps moving she will stay alive.

Today is my mother's birthday. She is ninety-five and she is all alone. She is alone anyway because the Covid-19 virus is keeping everyone isolated but today she is a little bit more alone because there is a big blizzard raging through the Northeast. Fifteen inches of snow have been promised. She assures me that she has heat and food and plenty to read. And as she reminds me, we still have the telephone. She is fine.

• This first English-language edition published in the United Kingdom in March 2022 by Les Fugitives • 91 Cholmley Gardens, Fortune Green Road, London NW6 1UN • www.lesfugitives.com • Cover design by Sarah Schulte • Photographs of Erica Van Horn's mother courtesy of the author • All rights reserved • No part of this publication may be reproduced, stored in a retrieval system or transmitted in any form or by any means, electronic, mechanical, photocopying, recording or otherwise, without prior permission in writing from Les Fugitives editions • A CIP catalogue record of this book is available from the British Library • The right of Erica Van Horn to be identified as author of this work has been identified in accordance with Section 77 of the Copyright, Designs and Patents Act 1988 • Text design and typesetting by MacGuru Ltd • Printed in England by TJ Books Ltd, Padstow, Cornwall • ISBN 978-1-7397783-0-9 • with assistance from *A Purse of Books.*

Les Fugitives is an independent press founded in 2014 to publish contemporary literary fiction and narrative non-fiction in translation from the French. In 2021, Les Fugitives published its first book originally written in English, *No. 91/92: notes on a Parisian commute* by Lauren Elkin. The modern classics and contemporary English originals collection 'the quick brown fox' provides a new framework for the publication of other Anglophone authors, including Erica Van Horn, Ruth Novaczek, and Etel Adnan.

In translation from the French, also published by Les Fugitives:

Eve out of Her Ruins and *The Living Days* by **Ananda Devi**
trans. Jeffrey Zuckerman

This Tilting World by **Colette Fellous**
trans. Sophie Lewis

Now, Now, Louison and *Nativity* by **Jean Frémon**
trans. Cole Swensen

Translation as Transhumance by **Mireille Gansel**
trans. Ros Schwartz

A Respectable Occupation by **Julia Kerninon**
trans. Ruth Diver

Little Dancer Aged Fourteen by **Camille Laurens**
trans. Willard Wood

Blue Self-Portrait and *Poetics of Work* by **Noémi Lefebvre**
trans. Sophie Lewis

Suite for Barbara Loden; Exposition, and *The White Dress* by **Nathalie Léger**
trans. Cécile Menon & Natasha Lehrer; Amanda DeMarco; N. Lehrer

The Governesses and *The Fool and Other Moral Tales* by **Anne Serre**
trans. Mark Hutchinson

Selfies by **Sylvie Weil**
trans. Ros Schwartz

• www.lesfugitives.com •